Reckless Ruby

This edition published in 1999 by Diamond Books
77–85 Fulham Palace Road,
Hammersmith, London, W6 8JB

First published in Great Britain by Andersen Press Ltd in 1992
First published in Picture Lions in 1993
Picture Lions is an imprint of the Children's Division, part of HarperCollins Publishers Limited,
77–85 Fulham Palace Road, Hammersmith, London W6 8JB

9 8 7 6 5 4 3 2 1

ISBN 0 261 67168-5

Printed and bound in Slovenia

Reckless Ruby

Written by Hiawyn Oram
Illustrated by Tony Ross

Once there was a little girl called Ruby. Ruby glowed like the jewel she was named after. People couldn't help noticing.

"Ruby is so beautiful!" they said. "Ruby is so precious!"

"Don't I know it!" said her mother. "Ruby is so precious I call her 'Precious'. Ruby is so precious I expect she'll grow up and marry a prince who'll wrap her in cotton wool and only bring her out for glittering banquets."

Ruby tried hard not to hear these dreadful predictions about her future. But they were made so often she couldn't help it and she went to see her friend Harvey for advice.

"You could try not being precious," said Harvey.

"But how?" said Ruby.

"By getting reckless," said Harvey.

So Ruby got reckless. Very, very reckless. She got so
reckless she told all the children on the playground that she
could fly . . .

. . . and had four stitches in her head because she couldn't.

"Oh Ruby! Precious baby!" wailed her mother. "If you don't take more care of yourself you're never going to grow up to marry a prince and get wrapped in cotton wool and only come out for glittering banquets."

"GOOD," thought Ruby . . .

. . . and got more reckless and said she could dance like a Russian acrobat on the bars of a moving bicycle . . .

. . . and had another four stitches in her head because she couldn't.

"Oh Ruby, Rubikins!" said her Granny. "Eight stitches and not even seven years old! If you don't take more care of yourself you are never going to grow up to marry a prince and get wrapped in cotton wool and only come out to give the servants orders."

"GREAT!" thought Ruby . . .

. . . and grew more reckless and ran away to sea and when the ship's captain found her she told him her father was really an ogre in a pin-stripe suit and her mother was a she-wolf in stone-washed jeans and on no account should he send her home or they'd eat her up. . .

. . . which caused Ruby's father to come home early from the office and get very, very cross.

"Ruby, this will not do," he said. "If you do not stop lying and start taking more care of yourself you will never grow up to marry a prince, which will be very, very disappointing for your mother and me."

"Sorry," said Ruby, lying again . . .

. . . and grew so reckless she said she could dive off any roof into a fishbowl . . .

. . . and dangle from skyscrapers by her shoelaces . . .

. . . and walk on water in lead boots . . .

. . . and cross the Cheddar Gorge single-handed . . .

. . . and eat fire,
      and swords,
            and porcupines . . .

. . . and climb into a python's cage
and shake hands with an octopus . . .

. . . and smoke five cheroots in the shrubbery without feeling sick . . .

. . . and spent six weeks in the children's ward because she couldn't. Or not without two broken legs, two black eyes, five fractured ribs, sixteen stitches, ten broken fingers, eight purple bruises and a very, very funny feeling in her stomach.

When her mother and father came to visit her they were
not very pleased.

"You are a very, very reckless little girl," they said.

"Not precious?" said Ruby.

"Not precious at all!" cried her mother.

"Not precious one bit?" said Ruby.

"Not precious one tiny, little bit!" snapped her father.
"Not precious enough to grow up to marry a prince and
be wrapped in cotton wool and only come out for glittering
banquets and to tell the servants what to do?"
"Certainly not!" wept her mother.
"Never!" wailed her father.

"WHEW!" said Ruby . . .
. . . and got better immediately and went to see Harvey.
"It's all O.K., Harv. I can stop being reckless and grow up."
"And marry me?" said Harvey hopefully.

"And be a fireman," said Ruby happily.

Hiawyn Oram was born and brought up in Johannesburg, South Africa. She graduated in English and Drama and acted professionally before moving to Britain. Since then, Hiawyn has had a variety of jobs in London – from cooking for film studios to writing television commercials. Tony Ross has collaborated with her on JENNA AND THE TROUBLEMAKER and ANYONE SEEN HARRY LATELY, as well as RECKLESS RUBY, and Satoshi Kitamura has also illustrated several of Hiawyn's books. She currently lives in London with her two sons, Maximilian and Felix.

Tony Ross was born in London in 1938. His dream was to work with horses but instead he went to art college in Liverpool. Since then, Tony has worked as an art director at an advertising agency, a graphic designer, a cartoonist, a teacher and a film maker – as well as illustrating over 150 books! Tony and his wife Zoë live in Macclesfield, Cheshire and have four children.